The Winter Mittens

The
Winter Mittens
Tim Arnold
Illustrations by the author

Margaret K. McElderry Books
NEW YORK

For Mom and Dad
T.A.

Margaret K. McElderry Books
Macmillan Publishing Company
866 Third Avenue
New York, NY 10022
Collier Macmillan Canada, Inc.

First Edition

Printed in Japan

10 9 8 7 6 5 4 3 2 1

Library of Congress Cataloging-in-Publication Data

Arnold, Tim.
The winter mittens.

Summary: Strange things begin to happen when
Addie puts on the old grey mittens she finds in an
unusual silver box.
[1. Mittens—Fiction.   2. Snow—Fiction.
3. Christmas—Fiction]   I. Title.
PZ7.A73794Wi 1988   [E]   88-2736
ISBN 0-689-50449-7

ddie was a small girl from a small city. She was smaller than most girls her age, and thin— but vigorous, not frail. She loved to run and skip and climb, so that she didn't seem small because she did things with such energy and skill.

Addie also had a kind heart. She was well liked by her classmates and tried hard not to speak badly of anyone. She was generous with her time and possessions and tried to do good things for others, as her parents had taught her.

She had long brown hair that she braided in warm weather and let fall free down her back in cold. She liked winter best because she could wear her long wool coat and scarf and crunch through the snow in her boots.

Addie was old enough, and her home close enough, to walk to school each day. She always took the same route and, because of this, knew every step of the way. She knew every crack in the sidewalk and every bump where the roots of trees were forcing up the concrete. She knew every house and the particular bark of every dog. Addie knew every store downtown, what was in the windows of each, and when even the smallest item was changed. She knew every brick, every trash can, every bush, tree, and shrub along the way. She could practically tell where in town she was without looking up from the sidewalk.

On a grey, cold day just between autumn and winter, Addie was on her way to school. As she passed the hardware store, her eye was caught by a flash of light. There was a space between the hardware store and the next building, too small to be an alley, where dried leaves and shreds of newspaper and other litter had been blown by the wind. From under the litter in the back corner of this space came the glint of polished metal, which Addie knew had not been there before.

She went into the space between the buildings, set her books down, and brushed away the dead leaves.

There lay a small silver box. It was a slim box, not more than an inch or two deep. On its lid and sides were engraved beautiful snowflakes of all shapes and sizes. It was clean and carefully polished, very different from its surroundings. And it was the loveliest thing Addie had ever laid eyes on.

She lifted the lid cautiously, expecting perhaps to find something inside more beautiful than the box. Instead, what lay in the blue velvet interior made her frown in puzzlement. It was an old pair of grey mittens, worn thin at the tips, with bits of yarn unraveling here and there.

"Why would anyone keep an old pair of mittens in such a lovely box?" she wondered.

Addie knew, somewhere inside her, that she ought to take the box to someone, perhaps one of the store owners, so that whoever owned the box could come and claim it. But there in the dim light, out of sight of people, Addie seemed to think differently.

"I certainly can't keep the silver box," she thought, "but I do need a pair of mittens."

She had lost her own and had not yet gotten new ones. Her hands were cold and were beginning to ache from holding the cold silver.

"Whoever left this here will come back for it. And they won't miss these old mittens, I'm sure," she told herself.

Addie tucked the mittens into her coat pockets and covered the silver box with leaves. Then she collected her books and hurried off.

As she neared school, the wind picked up. Addie's hands grew colder. She took the grey mittens from her pockets and slipped them on.

While she was crossing the last street before the school building, a snowflake drifted by. When she reached the school grounds, flakes were falling steadily. Children had gathered by the front doors, laughing excitedly about the first snowfall of winter. Addie joined in. Soon after, the bell rang and the children went in to their classrooms.

At recess they were disappointed to find that the snow had stopped before any had even accumulated on

the ground. Addie wrapped her scarf carefully around her neck, then took out the mittens and put them on.

Immediately a snowflake floated by. Followed by another. Then another and another and another. A cheer went up from the children. Addie stood still, staring at the mittens. Soon it was snowing steadily, big, soft, quiet flakes, spinning down and muffling the sounds of the children's games. Addie stood right in the same spot, first looking at the mittens on her hands and then at the falling snow. She remembered the engravings on the silver box and was sure that the snowfall was no coincidence.

When the bell rang ending recess, Addie quickly took off the mittens to see if what she thought would happen *would* happen.

As she lined up with the other children, the snow was letting up. By the time she walked through the doors, it had stopped altogether.

Addie could hardly sit still until school was out that afternoon, she was so anxious to try the mittens again. When the day finally ended, she hurried out of the

building. She waited until she was well away from the school, in case anybody should be watching, and took out the mittens.

Sure enough, the snow began to fall as soon as she put them on! Addie skipped down the sidewalk. What a wonderful thing she had discovered! But when she came to the place where she had found the box, she stopped skipping. Her stomach felt odd and she couldn't bring herself to see if it was still there, so she just passed by. Soon enough she was skipping again, and she left the mittens on all the way home.

At bedtime that night, Addie hid the mittens under her pillow. Her mother and father came and kissed her good-night. They shut the door softly behind them. Addie waited until the house was quiet and dark. Then she brought out the mittens, put them on, and tiptoed to the window to watch the snow come down.

The night was calm and still. No cars were out on the streets. Addie watched the pattern the snowflakes made as they passed through the glow of the streetlight.

"They just keep coming and coming," she thought

dreamily. She watched them until she grew too sleepy to stay up any longer. With the mittens still on, she climbed into bed and went to sleep.

When she woke the next morning, Addie jumped up and ran to the window. Clean white snow covered the ground and clung to the bare branches of the trees. The soft swirling flakes were still coming down. Addie heard the scrape of snow shovels on pavement. She heard the yells of children already out playing.

"That looks like enough for now." She smiled and took off the mittens. She put them under her pillow and went down to breakfast feeling quite pleased.

Over the next several weeks Addie used the winter mittens more and more frequently. Sometimes she put them on for just a few moments, sometimes for a few hours, and sometimes all night. Each time she used them she felt a little more pleased.

"People are so happy when it snows," she thought.

One day Addie amused herself by telling her friends she thought it looked like snow. Then she secretly slipped the mittens on inside her pockets and watched

their amazed faces as the first flakes fluttered down. She enjoyed that bit of deception but afterwards had an odd, hollow feeling in her stomach.

She got that same feeling when she thought of the silver box, but still couldn't bring herself to see if it was there under the leaves. More often than not she walked on the other side of the street and thought about something else as she went by.

"I'm sure," she told herself, "that the owner has come and found it by now."

Once it occurred to her that it might be the mittens rather than the box that were the more valuable. This thought she put quickly out of her mind, because she had come to think of the mittens as her own, as if she had always had them. Certainly she could not return them now.

"It's much too late," she thought. "And besides, everyone enjoys the snow so."

As Christmas drew near, Addie had an idea. She decided that she and the mittens would make these holidays the whitest in the city's memory.

"Everyone in the city will love this present, and no one but me will know where it came from," she thought, for Addie had not told a soul about the winter mittens, not even her mother or father. She always kept them hidden under her pillow or tucked away in her coat pockets when she was not using them.

On the day before Christmas, Addie spent the morning wrapping presents. Some of these she delivered to friends and neighbors, and the ones for her parents she placed under the Christmas tree. She cleaned her room carefully, and did all of the things around the house she had been asked to. Then Addie ran to her room while her mother and father continued with preparations for Christmas downstairs.

After putting on the mittens, Addie pulled a chair up to the window and watched excitedly as the snow began to fall once again. Before long it was coming thick and fast, adding to what had already accumulated over the weeks. It was a soothing sight to watch, so Addie sat in the chair all afternoon.

"I'll stay all afternoon and all evening and leave the

mittens on all night. I won't take them off till Christmas morning," she decided.

"It will be a lovely day," and she rubbed her mittened hands together. "Snow," she whispered, "snow!"

And the snow came down harder. It came down thicker and harder, until Addie could barely see the street from her window.

"Still," thought Addie, "I've seen more snow than this. Harder. Snow harder!"

Then the sky darkened and the snow began to swirl in gusts of wind. It came down harder and thicker still. Addie saw people hurrying along on the sidewalk, their faces wrapped with scarves, their backs bent against the wind. The street became completely covered—not a tire track could be seen. The few cars that passed slid and spun their way along, fighting both the wind and slippery snow. And it snowed still harder.

The sky went dark as night. The wind rattled Addie's windowpanes, and the snow was so thick that she could barely see the shape of the tree in her yard, not twenty feet away.

A car slid off the road just past the house. Its tires spun and whined, but it could not move. Finally its occupants got out and hurried away on foot. Addie stood up.

"Maybe this is enough," she said, looking worried. But when she pulled on the right mitten to take it off, it would not move. She tugged at the left one, but it wouldn't budge either. She pulled frantically at them with her teeth, but the winter mittens held fast to her hands, as if with a life of their own.

"Oh no!" she gasped. "What am I going to do now?"

The wind howled so loudly that it might have been in Addie's own room. She heard a cracking sound as limbs were torn loose from trees somewhere out in the storm. There was a loud explosion and a flash of blue light in front of the house. Addie's room went dark.

"Now the power is out. I *have* to do something," she thought. "The box! If I can find the silver box, maybe I can put the mittens in it."

Addie felt her way downstairs. She could hear her parents in the kitchen calling to her and getting out candles and matches.

They did not hear her put on her coat, scarf, hat, and boots and slip out the front door into the blizzard.

The sound of the wind outside was deafening. The snow stung Addie's cheeks and forehead. Her eyes watered when she looked up, so she just put her head down, leaned over against the wind, and shuffled ahead.

Even though she could see nothing, not even the familiar cracks in the sidewalk, Addie could sense where she was. She crept along, crossing streets and following the route she knew so well.

Her feet and hands grew numb, but the rest of her body was soon warm from the effort of fighting through the wind and snow. Addie reached downtown at last and felt her way along the storefronts until she came to the space between the two buildings where she had found the box.

The windblown snow was nearly waist deep there. Addie had to use her arms and legs to clear a path to the back corner where she had left the silver box. She dug and dug in the snow until she reached the frozen leaves and litter beneath. Then she pulled and scraped

away the leaves—and her hands hit cold, hard concrete. The silver box was not there. Addie's eyes filled with tears.

"It must be here somewhere," she sobbed.

She struggled back to the storefront. A strong gust of wind caught her and knocked her down. Snow went in her eyes and mouth. She got to her feet and ran wildly into the storm, no longer sure of her direction. Sometimes she bumped into a building or a trash can, but mostly she just put her head down and ran.

"I should have left that box alone," she cried. "I should just have left it. Now I'm lost and these horrible mittens will never come off. Oh help!"

Addie straightened up to see if she could tell where she was. As she did, the wind gusted and roared, swirling around and around her. Suddenly, the wind caught at the loose bits of yarn on the winter mittens and they began to unravel! The yarn was pulled up into the dark sky as the mittens furiously unwound themselves from Addie's hands. She watched openmouthed as the snake-like ends of the yarn disappeared up into the storm.

At that moment, the wind let up. The snow slowed. Within a few minutes the storm was over. Addie looked around. Here and there were abandoned cars, half buried. There were huge drifts that looked like gigantic waves, frozen as they crested. The power was still out and most houses were dark but for the faint light of candles.

Addie's blind run had taken her in the direction of her house. She saw now that she was not far from it. When she came within a block of her own home, she could hear her father's voice calling. She ran through the snow. She ran until she felt her parents' arms around her.

They took Addie into the house, where candles were lighting the darkened rooms. A fire was burning in their small fireplace. The three of them sat together in front of it, wrapped in blankets. She told them what happened as best she could, and they held her and said everything would be all right. After a while, Addie breathed a deep breath. A warm and good and whole feeling came over her.

The silver box and the storm and the winter mittens seemed small and long ago, almost like a dream. It was, after all, Christmas Eve.